HIS FLEEING WIFE

Arranged Marriage BWWM
Dark Mafia Romance

Jolie Damman

ISBN: 9798421895947
Imprint: Independently published

1st edition

Cover design by: Jolie Damman

CONTENTS

CHAPTER 1

The barrel rocking and shaking, I was relieved when it was finally put down on the floor. I was inside of it and I couldn't see anything around me. It was so dark that I couldn't even see my hands. My heart pounding in my chest, I had no idea where I was going. I had no idea where those people were taking me.

"A nice, big ass... That's what I'm talking about," someone in the room said, making me realize that they weren't Americans. Their language told me as much. Still, knowing that didn't help with anything. It wasn't like I could talk to them.

Not to mention that whoever was involved with this most likely wasn't someone I should ever get myself involved with, anyway.

I heard one of them coming to the barrel, making my heart race. I had no idea what was going to happen, and I was afraid of what might happen. I heard him put his hand on the barrel, for a moment not doing anything else.

"You won't be getting that anytime soon."

His hand started to pound against the top of the barrel, making loud noises inside of it. I widened my eyes as my mind started to think about all the possibilities. I was always like that. I was always thinking about everything.

"Huh?" The man asked, sounding confused about something.

"This feels hollow."

The other man came to us. "What do you mean, 'hollow'? It's probably fine. Just to put it there and move on."

I heard another pound against the barrel and the man said, "No, I mean. It's really more hollow than any other barrel I've hauled. This one is different."

"Stop messing around with it. We don't have all day."

His friend appeared to be annoyed and I still had no idea what was going to happen to me. I was in this barrel because I was fleeing from someone, and I never thought that my accomplice was going to betray me. I thought he was my friend, but he put me in this barrel. I didn't have any chance of escaping from inside of it.

"No, look. Do what I am doing." The man pounded against the barrel again, making me wish I could punch his face. If only he knew how much stress he was making me feel right now... It wasn't enough that I had been inside of this barrel for hours, now I had to put up with these guys, too.

I couldn't even scream. Duct tape over my mouth was impeding me from doing that.

"There's nothing wrong with this barrel." As soon as his friend said that, he banged his hand against the top of the barrel, stepping away from it. I couldn't see his face, but I could tell he was shocked by what he heard. He just noticed that the barrel was much hollower than it was supposed to be.

"See? I told you I wasn't lying."

"Something's really wrong with the barrel," he said, stepping back toward it.

I was feeling relieved. That they were thinking something was wrong with the barrel meant they were going to open it. When they opened it, they would realize I was inside of it and then they would take me out. At least, that's what I was hoping for.

I heard someone pulling out a gun, shivers running down my spine. They were probably thinking I was a spy hiding in here. They were probably going to shoot it first before opening it.

I tried to move my body however I could, but duct tape around my ankles and wrists prevented me from doing that. I couldn't even throw the weight of my body against the barrel. It was such a tight fit I was impressed they managed to put me inside.

The guys didn't say anything as one of them finally popped open the lid of the barrel. I looked up, fear on my face when I realized it was two Italian-looking men. I knew that their accents were different, but I didn't think I was in Italy. I thought I was still in America.

One of them pointed his gun at me, his eyes becoming tense.

"Who are you and what are you doing in the barrel?" He asked. I felt that if I didn't answer him right away, he wouldn't hesitate before squeezing the trigger.

His friend put his hand in front of the gun, saying, "Carlo, look. It's just a woman. I don't know what she's doing there, but she isn't a threat. She's all taped up."

His friend lowered his gun. "You're right, but she could still be dangerous."

"I don't think so. She wasn't trying to sneak into the country."

Of course not, I thought. Or at least, I wasn't trying to before someone knocked me out and put me in the barrel. My friend said he had a plan and that it was going to work, but that was before he did what he did. He betrayed me when I thought he was still the only friend I had in that house.

"It doesn't look like that's the case. She was put in here, probably for human trafficking."

"I think you hit the nail on the head."

My eyes went from one side to the other, realizing that these two men looked alike. They were probably brothers. Their hair was cut short, jet-black, they had thin lips, and stubble on their chins and jaws. Wearing uniforms fit for those that worked in the docs, I could tell they were nothing more than grunts.

That's why I wasn't as worried as I should be. If they were nothing more than grunts, then I could fight against them. I could overpower them. One of my friends, who was now dead, taught me everything I knew about judo.

"Carlo, I think I know what's happening here, and I don't know if we should bring this up to the Don."

"We'll think about that carefully. For now, we can't put her in the processing unit because I don't want to get our lives more fucked than they are."

"You're right. Let's first find out who she is."

As soon as he said that, the guy that wasn't Carlo took off the duct tape on my mouth. I could finally speak again, and I had a lot to say to them. The last thing I thought was going to happen was that I was going to be involved in a human trafficking ring.

"Please, get me out of here!" I said, feeling my throat dry. "They put me in here, and I don't know what's happening. I need to go back to my family."

Which was a lie. I was actually running away from my family. They were the ones who put me in this situation. I was fleeing from my husband.

"What do you mean? What happened before you were put in the barrel?" That was Carlo making those questions.

"I can't tell you. It's not safe. My husband is a very dangerous man and he would kill you."

He put his hands on his belly and started to laugh. "Your husband's dangerous? I don't think you know who we are."

When he was going to continue, his friend put his hand right in front of his mouth. "I don't think we should tell her anything about us." He looked back at me. "First, princess, I think you need to realize you are at our mercy. If you don't tell us what's really going on, then we'll be forced to tell the Don about you."

"I think that the Don probably already knows about this. There've been rumors that he was looking to expand his business. I guess that this is part of it. He's trafficking people."

I didn't know anything about that, but the operation they were running here wasn't something I wanted to get myself further involved with. I needed to get out of here as soon as possible.

"It looks like you two didn't know anything about it. Maybe you should just put something else in the barrel and let me leave. Your boss would be none the wiser."

"I don't think so, darling," Carlo said, trying to hit me with the grip of his gun when his friend stopped him again. As their eyes locked, I could tell that a crack was appearing in their friendship.

"Carlo, I'm not going to let you hit a woman. She's defenseless and needs our help."

"A soft heart, huh? And here I was thinking you actually deserved to be here with us."

His brother held his ground, his hand in front of him.

"It's not about that, but about doing the right thing."

"You are making a mistake."

"If you really think that way about it, then go tell the Don about this. Tell him that we now know about what he's really doing. I'm sure he'll like it."

A moment of tension, and I had no idea what was going to happen. All I was hoping for was them killing each other.

CHAPTER 2

Velio

Never had I thought that I was going to be involved in a human trafficking ring. I guessed that whoever put her in there must have thought that the drug was going to be enough. But it wasn't and she ended up waking up during transportation.

Carlo was still glaring at me like he was thinking about killing me. I knew that couldn't be the case, but the thought was still in my mind. For him, this work was the most important thing in the world. We weren't grunts in the mafia, but we weren't at the top level as well. That was reserved for the Don and the rest of his biological family.

Carlo eventually lowered his gun, turning away. "Then, what do you suggest we do with her? It's not like we can pretend she doesn't exist. They'll soon realize that something's wrong with us."

"Let's just keep transferring the other barrels."

"And if they also have more people in them?" He asked me with rage-filled eyes.

"If there are, then we'll deal with them. As long as it's just her, though, things will be simpler."

"I sure as hell hope you're right about that," he said, pulling up one of the barrels and putting it on the conveyor belt. He pressed the button on the side of the machine and it whirred to life. As soon as that second barrel was out of sight, he continued his work.

I turned and looked at the black woman in the barrel. It wasn't hard to figure out how she was feeling about this. Her eyes were telling me a part of it. She wasn't afraid. If anything, she was thankful we found out about her.

She was pretty, a sight for sore eyes. Long, dark hair, and honey-colored eyes. She'd be an important part of any man's dreams, and that was one of the reasons why I felt pity for her. I wouldn't have intervened if I didn't think that way about her.

It wasn't that I was thinking about taking advantage of her or anything like that, though. I just thought that someone so beautiful couldn't be dangerous to anyone.

"So, what are we going to do with her?" Carlo asked, putting another barrel on the conveyor belt. If those were hollow as well, he wasn't going to say anything. He was going to keep his mouth shut.

"I'm going to take her out of there and let her go. She isn't even from this country." Given her accent, I could tell she wasn't. She spoke like an American and looked like one.

I shouldn't be letting my feelings for her dictate what I should do, though.

"No, you won't. What do you think will happen when she gets out? How will she even leave this place without getting noticed?"

"With your help, I could," the woman said.

"No, you won't and we're not helping you either way."

Still, I couldn't help but feel that not helping her was a mistake. It was one thing working for the modern age mafia, and another finding out that we're helping them commit the worst crime in the world. I couldn't help but remember that this was all very reminiscent of slavery.

Why did they ship her off to Italy? Did they want her as cheap labor, or as something else? Sexual slave, perhaps? I didn't know, but the more I thought about it, the more I concluded I couldn't turn a blind eye.

"You should tell us everything you know," I said.

"Why? Do you think that will really change your mind?" I

could feel that her voice was changing, becoming weaker. I could tell she was going through a lot.

"I'm saying that we don't know anything about you, and Carlo would be more willing if he knew who you are."

"I don't know why I was put here."

"Bullshit," Carlo said, spitting on the floor. "Look at her. She isn't even phased that she's in a barrel. She knows what she's doing or, at least, she isn't so naive."

Carlo had a point, I thought, putting another barrel on the conveyor belt as I felt it wasn't hollow at all. I'd done terrible things in my life. Killing, robbing people, and piracy, but never kidnapped anyone and put them in a barrel. Whoever did that to this woman, they were cruel.

"The Don probably already knows about this. Nothing gets past him without his knowing. He's everywhere."

"He doesn't. That much I know. I'm just not about to let someone take advantage of her."

Carlo approached me, glaring at me. "You have a good heart, and it will be the downfall of you. We just climbed up the ranks recently. I don't want to fuck that up, especially over a black American girl."

I narrowed my eyes slightly. The way he said that hinted at something else, and I didn't want to think about it.

"I'm taking her out of there," I said, tumbling the barrel gently and then pulling her out.

"You're not going to do anything," Carlo shouted, shoving me away from her.

When I looked up, the woman was crawling on the floor. Carlo lifted his foot and was going to kick her stomach when I shoved him down against the floor. Putting myself on top of him, I pressed his arms against the ground so that he couldn't do anything else.

"Get off of me, idiot," he shouted, kicking me in the back.

I rolled off of him and stood up quickly when I realized that the woman was freeing herself. She cut the duct tape, tried going to the elevator, and when she pressed the button, I had to point my sidearm at her.

"You're not going anywhere."

"I told you she's more than meets the eye," Carlo said, grabbing his gun and going to her. "Look, someone will come here to check up on us. We need to keep working so that nobody suspects anything."

"You're right, and first we need to deal with her."

"We are going to have to tie her up again."

Carlo went over to her and was going to grab her wrists when she swung her leg over the ground, making him fall over. "Son of a bitch!" He shouted.

She was standing up when I realized her movement wasn't something I expected from someone who looked so defenseless. I sprinted over to her as she tried to punch me with her elbow. I dodged it and grabbed her from behind, immobilizing her.

"I'm trying to help you."

"I don't need anybody's help. I'm done needing help from anyone."

Just as she finished saying that, she grabbed my arms and pulled me up and over her so quickly it was over before I even realized what was happening. I fell harshly on the ground, my back in pain.

She was going to kick me when I grabbed her leg and yanked her, making her fall over on the ground as well. I propelled myself to be on top of her as I grabbed both of her arms and held them tightly.

"My help is everything you're going to get."

Just as I finished saying that, I heard the click of a gun by the side of my head. It was pointed at her, which made her stop struggling against me.

"I told you she's more than she wanted to make us believe she is. Are you going to trust your big brother this time?" He asked, huffing. Given the look in his eyes, I could tell he was pissed off that this woman beat him up.

To be honest, I was as surprised as he was about it. I never thought she was such a good fighter. Where did she learn those moves from, and what was her story? I asked myself, realizing that I was going to have to tie her up again. It wasn't something I wanted to do, but since it was obvious she wasn't just a victim, I needed to have time to think about what to do with her.

My brother handed me the duct tape, and I tied her up with it. I wasn't going to put her back in the barrel, but I was going to take her somewhere where we could interrogate her. I wasn't going to torture her, but I was pretty sure that the thought was in my brother's mind.

We took the elevator to the second floor, where nobody else was. Most of the time, we were alone here. He opened the door and I put her in the room, realizing that I was going to have to sleep on the floor in my brother's room.

She was a woman full of mysteries and I wanted to find out everything about them.

CHAPTER 3

Naida

Stuck inside the room, it was barely better than being in the barrel. At least they didn't tie me to the bed, which meant I could walk around in the room. It was dark, but at least it had a single lightbulb hanging from the ceiling. There was also a bed, a chair, and a sink.

Overall, I could see myself for a couple of hours in this place until I figured out what to do. I couldn't fight against those two men at the same time, but I could overpower one of them if he was alone. The problem was that I didn't think they worked here by themselves. There were probably more men outside and on the upper floors.

I was pacing from left to right when the door opened and in stepped Carlo. That was his name, or at least the name he used here. As he closed the door behind him, I realized he had a gun and was pointing it at me.

"Why are you here? Why are you alone? Do you think you can fight against me with just that gun?" I asked.

He scoffed. "You might have won against me when you were out of the barrel, but that only happened because I allowed it to. If it happens again, it will be much different."

"If you say so. Untie me."

He pulled the chair and sat on it. "I'm not going to do anything to help you. I'm here to ask questions and you're going to answer them."

"I'm not going to do that."

"Really? Do you really think you can get out of here on your own? Do you know how many men we have outside who could overpower you?"

"Your brother said he was concerned about me. He didn't think that his boss was involved in human trafficking. That's a serious crime, even in a country like Italy."

He stood up right away, striding toward me with his gun pointed at me. "What do you mean by that? Our boss is much better than that. He couldn't have known you were in the barrel, and he couldn't have known that someone was trying to sneak people into the country."

He had his gun pointed right to my head and I couldn't do anything. I could move, but I didn't think that would be wise. His brother was still on his side and I was pretty sure he would kill me if he had to.

"I was running away – or I suppose I should be saying I'm still running away from my husband. My name is Naida, and that's everything you need to know about me."

"Running away from your husband? How very interesting. Is he really that bad? Is he someone we should know about?"

"He's name is Elogio Doro and I'm pretty sure he's still looking for me. If you don't let me out of here right away, I'm sure he'll find me and he won't like it that you are keeping me locked up in here."

His eyes went wide when he heard my husband's name. "Elogio Doro… Yeah, I know that name. I've heard of him. I didn't know he married you."

"It happened behind closed doors, in his house. He didn't want anyone to know about it. I'm not really his wife," I said, looking down at the marriage ring on my finger. "I was his slave."

After a moment of silence, Carlo said, "Slave? Do you want me to feel pity for you? Given what I already know about you, I'd say you deserved it."

"You are a piece of shit. I wish I had kicked you."

"Next time, princess, you should try a lot harder," he said as he tried to hit me with his gun, but then the door reopened and his brother stepped into the room.

His eyes went wide when he saw me with Carlo. I didn't know what I should be feeling right now. Should I be feeling relieved that I wasn't alone with Carlo anymore? Should I be feeling afraid that I was with the same person that could match me in terms of how we fought?

I had no idea, but now I knew that my situation wasn't getting any better.

"Carlo, what are you doing here? I thought you were on the first floor like you said you were going to be."

"Well, I lied."

"Don't do that again. We need to stick together and trust each other."

His brother put his gun back into the holster. "I came here to find out more about her and she did tell me a couple of pretty interesting things."

"She did?"

"Yeah. She's running away from Elogio Doro, head of one of the most influential mafia branches in America. I never thought he was married to anyone, and much less that she was a woman as striking as her."

I didn't blush. Compliments weren't going to make me feel anything right now. More time spent here meant more time for my husband to find me. And if he did, I wouldn't get another chance. I wouldn't be able to escape from him.

Carlo's brother was the only one who probably had a good heart. If not that, then at least he could understand that I couldn't spend another minute in this place.

Elogio Doro was an Italian with a branching reputation. These grunts wouldn't do anything that he didn't like, unless they thought they could get away with it.

"Elogio? I'm shocked that he decided to get married. I thought he always said he wasn't looking for anyone."

"Must have probably thought he needed to extend his family to avoid his legacy from being ruined. After all, I heard that things are pretty rough in his operation. More and more of his subordinates are rising up and defecting."

That was true. It was one of the reasons why I managed to escape. I just never thought that my friend was going to betray me. I should never have trusted him.

"And her name is Naida. Pretty name for a black girl. She must really be something and worth a lot. But now that I'm thinking about it, it looks like nobody actually is expecting her here in the country. She was just running away," Carlo said, walking around me and making me feel uncomfortable.

He was dissecting me with his eyes, checking out every little part of me. I should be kicking him and punching him, but I wasn't going to.

His brother pushed him away from me, shouting, "Hey, what the hell do you think you're doing?"

"You know, Velio, sometimes I wonder what you're doing in the mafia."

"I'm here to help our family. Our parents need us."

"Not for much longer they won't."

"What do you mean by that?" Velio growled, growing tenser. I should be making use of the opportunity to run away from here, but the problem was not knowing what awaited me outside. What if the upper floors were teeming with men worse than these guys?

I couldn't take that chance. Not right now. Not to mention that it was going to take Elogio a lot of time to figure out that I was in Italy. And even then, it would take him longer to find out that I was here, wherever 'here' was.

"You know what I mean."

"I'm not letting you put a finger on her."

"You have such a good heart you make me envious."

Velio narrowed his eyes. I could feel the sparkles flying between their eyes. Carlo was the less respectable brother, the one willing to get his hands dirty. Velio, on the other hand, was the guy who was doing this because he didn't have another choice. It wasn't that he was being forced to, but that he couldn't see another way out of this.

"Get out of here."

Carlo didn't say anything, slightly tipping up his chin.

"Fine, but I'll be back. She's running away from Elogio and doesn't have anyone in Italy waiting for her. That means she's fair game."

"You should go look elsewhere."

"Wow, I didn't think she was softening up your heart even more than it already is. I'm impressed. She really is something else. I can't help but wonder what she'd feel like riding on my dick."

Having said that, his brother opened the door and walked out. As we heard his fading footsteps, Velio turned and said, "You need to cooperate. I'm the only one here willing to help you."

And I couldn't help but feel a little connected to him, now that he said that. I never thought there was anyone in the Italian mafia with a good heart.

Perhaps I was in luck.

CHAPTER 4

Velio

Opening the door to her room, I felt something hard hitting against my face as I fell over backward on the floor. I snapped my head up as I realized it was Naida who had done that. She punched me in the face with her elbow and was now leaping out of the room.

I stood up and went after her as she started to sprint down the corridor. She didn't know anything about this place and I had the upper hand when it came to that. I was surprised by her speed, her hair flowing behind her head.

My face still stung, but I ignored it. She turned to the right and stopped when she realized she hit a dead end. I was huffing slightly as I approached her.

"I was trying to help you, but now I realize I was wasting my time. I should've put you back in the barrel."

"Maybe you should've done that." And as she said that, she assumed a fighting stance.

"I don't want to fight you."

Naida dashed toward me, swinging her arm and trying to hit me with her leg, but I grabbed her from behind like last time. I pushed the weight of my body against the floor, this time making sure that she couldn't pull off the same trick.

I could feel my groin pressing against her ass, and I couldn't help but feel that it really was a nice ass. No wonder my brother was drooling over her. Naida was a woman like no other. Strong-spirited, willing to fight, and in pretty good shape.

She was struggling against me, but it wasn't going to be enough. I was holding her tightly against me. I wasn't going to make the same mistake.

"Look, I really don't want to make this harder than it needs to be. I want to help you as much as I can."

"I can't even trust you. As far as I'm concerned, you're like everyone else."

"Look, I can let you do something. Do you want to take a shower?"

Hearing that, she stopped struggling against me. I supposed that the thought of taking a shower was very tempting.

I could smell her body and something about it was making my dick stir in my pants. I wasn't doing this because I was trying to take advantage of her, but I couldn't deny she was a very gorgeous woman.

"You are pulling my leg. You're not going to let me take a shower. You just want me locked up in that room so that you don't have to worry about me."

"That's not it. I want to help you because I don't want to see you suffering. I want to get you out of here, but I don't know how to do that without drawing attention to us."

After a moment of silence, she said, "Alright, I want to take a shower. It's been such a long time that I'm stinking."

I wasn't going to say that she was. I wasn't about to ruin something beautiful that we were already building on. Perhaps 'beautiful' was too strong of a word, but there was no denying that it was there.

"I'm going to take my arms off of you and if you try anything stupid again, I won't hesitate."

"You have my word," she said, again making me wonder the kind of woman she really was. She hadn't been born in an environment where she was docile and innocent. She knew what hardship was like and that she had a tough upbringing.

I slowly took my arms off of her, stepping away from her to be on the safe side. I didn't point my gun at her even though part of me was begging me to do that.

As she slowly turned around, I couldn't help but dissect her body with my eyes. Her curves, her hair, her eyes, and even her nose – everything about her was perfect.

And I could tell she felt something similar regarding me. I didn't want to build false hope about it, but there was no denying that the thought was in my mind. Maybe I'd been in this place for too long. It was almost like a bunker.

"Well, take me to the bathroom."

I waved my hand. "After you. I'm going to guide you."

She narrowed her eyes slightly as she went ahead, turning to the left when I asked her to. We walked along several corridors until we reached the bathroom.

I opened the door as I said, "Sorry, but I don't have a change of clothes for you."

She sniffed her armpits as she said, "That's okay. I've smelled worse before."

If we were more intimate, we would be laughing at her comment, but nothing like that happened. She entered the bathroom and closed the door. I leaned on the wall as I closed my eyes. It looked like nobody was in the vicinity, which meant she should have enough time to take her shower.

I heard the water falling from the shower head in the bathroom as I imagined her naked. Gosh, I was so desperate to get laid again, wasn't I? I curled up the corner of my lips as I wondered what it would feel like to be on top of her, thrusting my hips against her ass over and over...

I thought I heard a pair of footsteps coming from the other side of the corridor, but when I reopened my eyes and looked there, I couldn't see anything. Must have been my imagination, I thought.

I heard Naida putting her clothes back on and then she opened the door, stepping out of the room. I raked her body with my eyes, realizing that it was too obvious what was happening. A woman as strong-willed as her probably noticed that and was planning on how she could use it against me.

Nevertheless, I wasn't worried. It wasn't like I thought she could win in a fight against me, after all.

She looked so much better now after taking a shower. Her hair looked smoother, her skin brighter, and her smell so much better, too. Everything about her was making me think about how much I wanted to have her for myself.

"Thanks for the shower, but you're not fooling me." As soon as she finished saying that, she swung her leg and hit me right on my stomach, making me fall over backward again.

I stood up right away as I dashed after her. She turned left and then right as she hit another dead end.

I was shaking my head as I remembered what I was thinking. I thought we were bonding. I thought we were starting to understand what we thought. I thought we were going to help each other out.

"I tried to help you," I said, swinging my arm upward as I hit her in her stomach hard enough to make her gasp. It hurt me that I had to do this against her, but there was no helping it. "And you're going to need more than yourself to beat me. Maybe my brother was right about you."

"Your brother is nothing more than an asshole. I hope you realize that one day."

I furrowed my eyebrows. I didn't like it when people bad-mouthed my brother, and I wasn't going to take that kindly from a stranger.

"I'm going to take you back to your room and then tomorrow I'll figure out what to do with you."

She stood up slowly with her hand still on her belly.

"I never thought you were better than the person you are. You're nothing more than a mob grunt. You're nothing more than trash. I hope you can live with that for the rest of your life."

I grabbed her arm and started to take her to her bedroom harshly. "You don't know anything about me."

"You're not difficult to figure out. You are just like my husband. You are as violent as he is. You're hurting me."

I really was. I was gripping her arm quite tightly and I wasn't easing it. When we reached the door, I opened it and tossed her into the room. She fell over on her side as she glared at me with hatred-filled eyes. I knew what was going on in her mind. She wanted to kill me and make me regret my choices.

But little did she know that I was already regretting them. I shouldn't have felt pity for her. I should've done what my brother said. I should have kept her in the barrel and pretended that we hadn't seen her.

I closed the door with a loud thump as I went back to my brother's room. I should've tied her up, but I wasn't in the mood to do that right now. I was going to ask my brother to do it for me.

What a shitshow this whole thing was.

CHAPTER 5

Naida

If he was thinking that being nice to me was going to work, he had something coming. He was so stupid that he forgot to tie me up. The next time they opened the door, I was going to be right behind it and I was going to kill whoever was on the other side. That much I was already promising to myself. They had no idea the kind of things I had to go through with my husband. He always wanted me as his sex slave.

Before meeting him, I was nothing more than a flower who didn't know anything about the darker sides of life.

My family made me marry him. The reason behind that was pretty simple. They needed more money to fuel their operations, and he was the only one willing to fulfill their request. When they had his money, they even stopped remembering that I existed.

The whole thing was such a mess that even now I didn't like thinking about it.

I opened my eyes when I thought I felt something moving in the room. Lying in the bed, I couldn't see or hear anything, though. I didn't think much of it and tried to turn. Maybe I could sleep again, but I wasn't holding my breath. I wasn't someone who could sleep well easily, and it showed. I hadn't looked at myself in a mirror since escaping from Elogio's mansion, but I was still pretty sure that the heavy bags under my eyes were worse now.

Minutes later, I was finally falling asleep again when I felt something moving in the room. I sat up straight on the bed right away, my heart pounding. Why did it look like the room was bigger now than before?

I didn't know the reason why I was feeling that way about it, but something looked off about this. Either someone was in the room, or the air swirl meant that something else was happening. Perhaps it was a crack in one of the walls letting through the air. Whatever it was, I needed to stop it. I couldn't fall asleep otherwise.

And yes, I was pretty sure something was going on. There couldn't be another explanation. I wasn't going crazy or creating weird theories in my mind.

I didn't say anything like in those corny horror movies where the heroes and the heroines died. Instead, I remained where I was. I wasn't making any noise here and it was unlikely that, assuming there was another person here, they knew I was defenseless.

Just when I felt the air moving around me all of a sudden and I tried evading it, a hand jumped out of the darkness and grabbed my neck, shoving me down against the bed. I gasped, a face soon appearing in front of me.

The face of a man I knew well.

Carlo. I knew him well enough.

I didn't know anything about his family other than that his brother was a bigger asshole than he thought he was. I didn't know if they still had their extended family, issues unresolved, and that sort of thing, but I knew that he wasn't someone to be messed around with. Not to mention that the rage in his eyes told me that something else was at play here.

He was thinking about hurting me.

I heard him unbuckling his belt and taking it off. What the fuck? I struggled against him, but if there was something I wasn't better than him at, it was strength. He was just stronger than me, and he kind of caught me off guard, too.

"What are you doing?" I asked through gritted teeth. I couldn't put into words how much I hated him, even though I didn't know him well. The fact that he was pulling his pants down now and looking at me with those eyes could only mean one thing, and I didn't like it.

I was afraid of it, to be more precise.

"I've been thinking about this since my little dip shit of a brother thought that keeping you here with us was a good idea," he said, now lowering his underwear, too.

I couldn't believe that he was going to rape me! I wasn't going to let him, but that was a new low, even for someone like him. His fingers were digging so deep into my skin that he was hurting me, and I was finding it more and more difficult to breathe.

"This isn't something you can ever walk away from," I said, trying to strike him with my knee, but it was impossible. He just blocked it with his knee, opening a devilish smile.

I could see his teeth clearly in the darkness.

"Sorry, little princess, but I've got other things on my mind right now," he groaned, ripping the shirt off of my body and fumbling my breast. He didn't even know how to do it properly. I didn't think he got laid often.

"I'm going to fucking kill you, asshole," I said, his fingers digging deeper into my neck and making me feel like he was going to rip open one of the arteries. Now that I was thinking about it, that would be preferable to letting him rape me. And it didn't matter how much I struggled, he was still going on with it and it didn't look like anyone was going to come to my rescue.

"I'd love to see you try but, princess, that isn't going to happen," he said, now ripping my pants off and brushing his finger over my panties. He flipped me around on the bed, positioned himself behind me, and I didn't know what else I could do.

It was like the way he was gripping my neck was fading all the strength I had to fight him.

When I thought that all hope was lost, the door opened all of a sudden and someone stepped into the room. Knowing that I was in this place, I knew it couldn't be anyone who was actually coming to help me. If anything, he was going to help Carlo with raping me.

But he then grabbed Carlo by his shoulder and yanked him

away from me. I sat up on the bed right away and then jumped off of it, landing hard on the floor.

When I heard his voice, I knew that things were going to be better. I didn't trust him at all, but there was no denying he felt some sympathy for me.

"Carlo, what the hell are you even doing?" Velio shouted, his voice reverberating in the room.

Carlo put his clothes back on, pointing his gun at his brother.

"I was just having some fun."

"By raping her? That's who you turned into? I never thought you had fallen so low."

Carlo tsked. "You don't know anything about me. This whole time we've been living together, you still think the same way. You never learn. You're still going to get this so deeply fucked for being the way you are."

Velio shook his head. "It doesn't matter what you say to me. I'll never forgive you for trying to rape her, and she needs our help."

Carlo waved his finger left and right. "Don't put that on me. You are the one trying to help her. I'm here just for the money, like everyone else. You would do well to keep that in mind."

"You're such a piece of shit and I hate you so fucking much," Velio growled and a fight broke out, both grunts punching and kicking each other.

When they were completely bruised and spent, Carlo walked out of the room saying, "This doesn't end here. I can promise you that much."

"You can do whatever you want, but I'm going to be staying here outside the door to make sure she's safe."

He holstered his gun as he looked at me. Everything was such a whirlwind in my mind that I stepped away from him when he approached me. He held up his hands as if he was trying to say that he came here in peace.

"I'm different from my brother. I won't hurt you."

"After what he tried to do, I'm not taking any chances. Step out of the room and leave me alone," I said when I felt my body bumping against the wall.

"You're hurt. Let me help you. I have some medical experience."

"It's not that bad."

"After what happened today, do you really want to keep behaving like that? Or don't you want to have at least someone helping you?"

I knew that I shouldn't accept it, but the way he put it... It made all the sense in the world to me. And so, I nodded and sat back down on the bed.

CHAPTER 6

Velio

I came back into her room with a first aid kit in my hand. I closed the door after checking the outside to make sure that Carlo wasn't going to come back. I didn't need to go back to where the conveyor belt was because we were on our break.

I popped open the first aid kit as I sat down on the bed. The light of the room was turned on and I could see her face perfectly. Her face was still as beautiful as I knew it was, but her neck was hurt. I could see the red marks where my brother's hand was gripping it.

Seeing that, I couldn't help but feel rage bubbling up in my veins. I wanted to hurt him, which was something that never happened to me before. I never felt this way about my brother.

Looking at her again, I couldn't help but notice she was a couple of years younger than me.

"How old are you?" I asked, looking at her eyes. She was strong and determined, but there was no denying that what happened deeply affected her. It was a memory that was going to forever be in her mind.

"Does my age even matter? I'll be out of here soon. That's a promise I'm making to myself."

I was treating the wound of her neck as I said, "Maybe it doesn't matter that much, but I still want to know. After helping you, don't you think that's something I deserve, at least?"

I was holding a ball of cotton which had been coated in an alcoholic substance. It should work to make her wounds feel better, I thought.

It was the first time I was being this intimate with her, which was more exciting than what I was showing on my face. I wasn't using this moment to take advantage of her, but I couldn't deny that she made me feel something different for her.

Perhaps it was the fact that I had been alone for so long here I forgot what it was like to hold a woman in my arms.

We locked our eyes for a moment and it was different than all the other times we looked at each other. Maybe I was wrong about it, but I could kind of feel she thought the same way about me.

"I'm not going to tell you what my age is, and that's not something you should even ask a woman, anyway."

"You're right. I shouldn't have asked." I chuckled, dabbing the cotton to one of the marks on her skin again, seeing her face contort slightly as she felt a little bit of pain.

"Does it hurt? Are you feeling better already?"

"I'm fine. He didn't even hurt me that bad. I'm only letting you treat me because you asked nicely."

"Well, I'm happy I can help you. I really feel sorry for you. I mean, we found you in a barrel and if I hadn't been curious about it, you would have been shipped off God knew where. I can't imagine what you must've gone through."

I looked at her eyes again, realizing that there was a certain understanding between us. It was like she was finally realizing I wasn't the bad man she thought I was.

"I was running away from my husband, like I told you. I need to get out of here as soon as possible before he figures out what's happening."

I put my hand on top of hers, feeling how soft her skin was.

"It doesn't matter what he does. If he finds out that you're here before I figure out what to do, I'll help you. I will stand between you and him."

She held my gaze for what felt like an eternity. Being this close to her meant that I could smell the smell of her body, and it was arousing me even more than I already was. I couldn't stop stealing glances at her lips, wondering what it would feel like if I kissed her.

And the thing was that I could tell she was feeling the same way, too. She didn't move her hand away from mine when I put it on top of hers. It was like she was welcoming my sympathy.

"And why are you trying so hard to help me? I don't understand. I'm nothing more than a stranger to you."

"I don't know. When I see someone who doesn't have anything to do with this, I just feel this urge to help them. Maybe my brother is right about one thing at least. Maybe having such a good heart will be my downfall."

"You know what? Your brother is so stupid he can't see that it's actually your biggest strength. He could learn how to be a better person from you."

When she said that, when I was looking into her eyes, I felt like there was a force pulling me down. I was leaning into her, the smell of her body stronger, and we were almost going to kiss.

My heart was pounding slightly. I wasn't nervous, but I had no idea if this was something I should be doing. I told myself several times before that I didn't want to take advantage of her.

And I wasn't. I was falling in love with Naida, if that was even her real name. I was saying that because there was a good chance it wasn't.

But then she pulled her head back suddenly. I was left confused about what was happening. I continued to treat the wound on her neck, though, feeling that my body was a little sweaty now.

I couldn't deny that she just did something I never thought would happen. She told me she was falling in love with me as well.

Minutes later, I closed the first aid kit and stood up. I was holding it in my hand as I said, "I asked my brother to tie you up to the chair, but I don't think that's necessary anymore. And don't worry – I'm going to be outside in case he shows up again."

She shook her head, smiling gently.

"Thanks."

I walked to the door when she said. "Don't you want to stay a little while longer?"

"I thought you hated me."

"I still kind of do, but I can see you're much different than all the mafiosos I know. You have a good heart."

I turned around, putting the first aid kit back on the floor. I stepped over to her and sat back down on the bed. We locked our eyes for no more than a second before we kissed, and this time I put my hand on the back of her head to make sure she wasn't going to escape this time.

Her lips were as sweet as I thought they were, and our kiss was very passionate and slow. We were savoring the moment second by second. We were washing away all the bad memories we had in our minds. She was finally loosening herself up.

I broke the kiss as I looked into her eyes.

"Well, suffice to say I never thought this was going to happen."

She chuckled. "I thought the same, but then I realized you were right about something."

Feeling curious, I asked, "Are you going to tell me what I was right about?"

She moved her hand around my neck, as if she was trying to tell me she didn't want me to go anywhere.

"That it's much better to have a friend here – or at least someone I care about – than to be alone."

Hearing that, I couldn't help but pull her to me for another hot kiss, our lips connecting once again. The kiss was as passionate as the one we had before and, this time, we even battled using our tongues. It was also a very slow kiss and as time went by I realized it was going to be difficult to part ways with her.

"You kiss so well. I'm going to miss it," I purred, wishing I could make this moment last for a long while.

"Let's make the most of it, then." When she finished saying that, she stood up and went to the door. I gave her the key and she closed it. When she turned around, I was already all over her, pinning her against the door.

Her eyes bulged as she realized how hungry I was for her. I took the shirt off of her body as I promised that this was only going to end one way. After all the shit Naida went through, I was going to give her an unforgettable night.

I was going to make her happy, even though I didn't think it was going to be anything more than a fling.

CHAPTER 7

Naida

He pushed me back against the bed, his hands pulling off my bra like it was nothing. My breasts were exposed. Given the look on his face, I could tell he was loving what he was seeing. This wasn't the most romantic environment for a one-night stand, but that was okay. I'd been in worse places and had had sex with worse people, my 'husband' included. I didn't even know if I should still be calling him my husband. I supposed it didn't matter right now anymore.

He was on top of me, peppering me with kisses that were impossible to control. Perhaps it was the fact that I'd been so stressed this whole time that was finally doing it. I was letting my guard down for someone that was treating me so well.

And in the life I'd had, it was something remarkable. Most other people, Carlo included, just wanted me for my body.

I kissed his lips again and he murmured into my ear, "You're gorgeous." Him saying that was one of the upsides of him being the good-natured man he was.

His hands roamed over my body as he cupped one of my boobs. He pressed his fingers against it and then brushed his finger against one of my nipples. I moaned, thinking about what he was going to make me feel when he was inside of me. I was pretty sure he was thinking the same thing, too.

His body was warm, sweat pooling on his forehead. I moved

my hands around his shape as he finally took off his shirt. What he said before about not being such a good person was true. He had tattoos on his chest, and one of them was the symbol of his mafia gang. I couldn't help but wonder what some of his other tattoos meant, but I didn't have time to ask.

Groping his muscles, I felt what could only be scars on his skin. It made me wonder about the kind of life he had – and still was having – thanks to him being in the mafia. It made me wonder about his past, and I couldn't help but feel like asking him those questions when we had time for that.

But time was something that I just didn't have. I moved my hand down and got rid of his belt. He pushed his pants down and kicked them away. My hand brushed over the front of his groin, and I felt his cock.

Gosh, it was immense, and I wondered if it was even possible to fit it inside of me. After being with someone so violent like Elogio, I was savoring this moment for everything that it was. I couldn't wait until he was fitting that thing inside of me and saying sweet things into my ear as he fucked me.

He groaned against my lips as he made his way down, peppering my neck with several extra kisses. When he was loving my belly, he stopped as he allowed me some time to catch my breath.

It was just about enough time to make me feel that I wasn't going to pass out.

I ripped off his underwear when I felt that this couldn't be delayed any longer. Wrapping my fingers around his shaft, I started to pump it slowly and nicely. I needed to feel how big he really was. Given what I could feel, I wasn't disappointed, I thought with a sly smile on my face.

"It's too much," I groaned, his tongue licking my little nub as he continued to make love with me.

"Don't worry. This is just the start," he promised as he took his dick into my mouth and let me give him a nice, slow blowjob. I closed my eyes and focused on the underside of his dickhead, giving him as much pleasure as I could.

He tilted his head backward and allowed me to take hold of

him. I felt his legs with my hands as I deep-throated him. When I was all the way down and could feel his balls against my chin, I pulled my head back up. His dick was throbbing when I did that.

I kissed the tip of his dick and gave it a nice, slow stroke as he flipped me around on the bed. He climbed on top of me after putting on a condom. I was a little disappointed that he was doing it with protection, but there wasn't anything I could do about it, and it wasn't wise, either.

Velio pulled me to him strongly as he penetrated me with his hard cock. I felt it breaching through every barrier and when he finished filling me with it, I felt like I was losing my virginity all over again.

His hands were holding me as he asked, "Everything okay, dear?"

"Yes," I breathed, his thrusts starting only seconds after that. He was pounding in and out of me moments later, and I could tell he wasn't going to last long.

His pace increased further as he rammed in and out of me. When he went still and his dick started to convulse inside my cunt, my walls clenching him, I felt an intense orgasm exploding in my mind.

I came with him and then he pulled out. He tossed the used condom somewhere in the room and then came back to me. I thought that he was going to lie down with me and then spoon me, but he picked up his clothes and put them back on.

I covered myself with the thin bedsheet as I wondered what was going on in his mind. When he put his pendant on his neck again, I asked, "You're leaving already?"

"I've got something I need to do. I wish I could stay a while longer, but… I can't. I think I know how to get you out of here. I'll be back tomorrow morning."

I couldn't help but groan, part of me wishing things were different. I was thinking that way about it probably because I missed being in a man's arms. I missed feeling someone's warmth and it sucked that I couldn't do those things now.

But Velio was right about one other thing. What we had was

nothing more than a one-night stand, and it was going to remain that way for the rest of my life. I should be looking forward to the new life I was going to have in Italy. It was going to be amazing. It was a good thing I knew the language.

He went out of the room and closed the door, leaving me alone with my thoughts. I started to think about all the bad things that could happen while he was away, and I couldn't help but stand up and already prepare myself for any eventuality. I didn't have anything with me, but I had my strength and wits.

Carlo was the only one who knew about me. If he was outside looking for another opportunity to strike, now was the right time for that. The seconds were passing and they were so slow. It was almost like time was playing tricks on me.

I shook my head, standing up and staring at the door as I tried to hear any incoming footsteps. But there weren't any footsteps coming in this direction. The environment outside of the room was so silent I'd be able to hear a pin dropping to the floor.

When minutes passed and I realized that nothing of the sort was going to happen, I sat back down on the bed and started to remember the amazing moment I had with Velio. He was so good. He made me feel loved and like a woman again.

I was stressed out for so long with my husband I forgot what those things felt like. I sighed, lying on the bed when the door opened all of a sudden. The first thing I thought was how in the world I didn't realize someone was already coming here.

I couldn't see his face, but it was pretty evident it was someone who knew me well. He stepped into the room as I realized he had a smile on his face. He was looking at me.

He wasn't alone, either. He was with a group of men who had their guns pointed at me. It couldn't be Velio, but it could be his brother. Turning my eyes to the left, I wasn't surprised when I realized it was him, and he had a look of satisfaction on his face.

"Sorry, princess, but I had to tell my boss about you, and then he showed me he was already in contact with your husband. He was worried about you. He's still worried about you. He's been looking for you this whole time."

I didn't say it, but I imagined that he was going to be paid handsomely for that information. Carlo was such an asshole. He sold me off and now I didn't know what was going to happen to me.

A tear rolled down my cheek. I thought I was going to have a lot more time.

CHAPTER 8

Velio

I couldn't believe what happened and I wasn't going to let things end that way. That was why I was already marching to my car. My brother was behind me. He grabbed my shoulder and pulled me until I turned around. He tried to hit me with his fist, but I dodged it.

I punched him in his face as I said, "I should be locking you up in the worst prison we have in the country. You're the worst person I know. I can't believe you went behind my back like that."

"You should be thanking me that the boss didn't kill you right then and there. I spoke on your behalf and I convinced him. You're only alive now because of me."

I shoved my finger against his chest. He palmed his cheek as he felt the intermittent pain coming from where I hit him.

"I should kill you right now for trying to rape her. Maybe I should even tell the boss about that. I'm sure he wouldn't stand it."

"He doesn't have to know anything. Besides, it's not like he really cares about it."

I took a deep breath, running my hand over my face.

"Did you find out if he knew about it, that he was smuggling people into the country in the barrels?"

"No, I didn't pay much attention to that. Frankly, I was thinking about something else. Someone found a used condom in the room, right when you walked out of there and went to do something else. It's gross that I'm saying this to you right now, but I think it belongs to you. This whole time, you were just trying to get under her pants…"

"That's not it. It just happened. And she asked for me to stay a little while longer with her. I should've listened to her."

After a moment of silence, he affirmed, "Don't hit me again. I'm your brother. We're supposed to stick together." He glanced at my car. "Where do you think you're going right now?"

"Where do you think, rapist? To find and save her. I'm not letting that asshole put his hands on her again. She told me everything that happened while she was with him, and I don't want to leave her helpless."

Carlo chuckled. "Given how well she fought against us, I don't think she'll be defenseless. I'm going with you."

I shut the door of the car.

"No, you're not coming. This is the perfect place for you. Away from everything, where you never get a chance to have sex with anyone."

He sighed, putting his hand on the door of the car.

"You realize that this is treason, right? The men upfront won't let you out. They'll shoot you. Even if they don't manage to kill you right away, they'll hunt you down until they do."

"I think I'm willing to take the risk."

He didn't say anything else, letting a minute of silence take place between us.

"I didn't think you were going to fall in love with that woman. I don't even remember her name anymore. She was never important to me."

"It's Naida, and you're not going to change my mind about this. I'm going either way." I glanced at the men by the front gate. We were having a loud argument, but that was okay. Nobody could hear us. They didn't know I was planning on barging through.

"Okay, and say you actually manage to find where she lives – as far as I'm concerned, you don't even know that, too. Then, what? What will you do? Will you kill everyone where she lives and get her out of there? How many people do you think will come after you two?"

"It's a risk I'm willing to take," I said, shoving the trunk of the car closed. I was bringing as many guns with me as possible. Assault rifles, submachine guns, pistols, and even grenades. They were all from this place where we processed the barrels left by the ships. I looked beyond the building and couldn't help but feel a sense of peace about the place. The slow crashing waves truly made it beautiful with the rocky cliff sides.

"You're making a huge mistake," he shouted, shoving his finger to my face and putting himself between me and the front door. I didn't want to have to fight him, even though the only thing he deserved right now was to be beaten up to a pulp. I should be telling my boss about what happened when Carlo and Naida were alone. If only our boss hadn't already left…

"Get out of my way," I barked, happy that everyone else was so far away from us they couldn't hear anything. Not even a peep of this argument. Knowing that allowed me to feel as free as I wanted to be right now.

"Or what?" He said, crossing his arms over his chest.

"Or you'll force me to do something I don't want to," I growled, putting myself right in front of him. I could smell the stench of cheap beer coming from him, and I didn't like it at all. It made my stomach churn. If there was something I didn't like, it was people accepting less than what was the best. I used to drink, too, but only the better brands – the ones that were actually worth my money and time. I didn't like the knockoffs that thought they were denting the market.

I thought we were going to fight again. It would be just like Carlo to do something like that, but instead he uncrossed his arms and moved away from the car.

"Good luck. You'll need it."

"You won't sell me off like you did with Naida, right?"

He chuckled, opening a devilish smile. "No. Nobody knows about this. I know you'll die anyway. There's no point telling anyone about it."

I studied him for a couple of seconds as I wondered if he was telling me the truth or not. Realizing that I couldn't waste any more time, I opened the door of the car and sat down.

One thing that he said did make some sense, though, and it was the fact that I had never before felt something so strong for a woman. I was willing to go through with this until the end.

After what she told me, I wanted to make sure she was going to be okay, and that couldn't happen as long as she was with her husband.

I fired up the engine of the car before accelerating it, the guards at the front gate turning around as they realized something was wrong. I was speeding up the car even though the front gate was still closed. My eyes narrowing, I was focused on only one thing – figuring out if what I felt for Naida was true love. I supposed that was something I'd know only when I was with her again.

"Open fire! He's not going to stop," one of the guards shouted as he realized it was already too late. Seconds later, I was crashing through the front gate like it was nothing.

I felt the car swerving and losing the direction I was trying to follow, but after turning it slightly to the left, the problem was fixed. I looked behind my shoulder as I saw the guards getting into their cars and scheming over their earpieces.

They were already telling the boss about what was happening. My heart was in my throat because I realized I was never coming back here. I lived most of my life in this place and I wasn't just abandoning it. I was also abandoning my country.

My boss's influence was far-reaching and I was pretty sure he could find me anywhere he wanted, including the United States.

Regardless, I was going there and upon reaching the city where Naida said she was going to be, I'd hunt for Elogio's mansion. I was pretty sure I was going to find it. It should actually be one of the easiest things about this. After all, he made no efforts in hiding himself from the authorities.

I already even had a plan. I was going to disguise myself as one of his guards and then I was going to find my... the woman I couldn't stop thinking about. Then, I'd get her out of there and

we'd figure out what to do.
I just couldn't wait until I had her in my arms again.

CHAPTER 9

Locked up in my room, naked and chained to a wall, I had no idea what my husband wanted me to do. My throat was dry. It had been a long time since he gave me something to drink, and if I wasn't confused about it, the last thing he gave me was his own piss. Just remembering that I probably drank his piss was making my stomach churn.

I wanted, most of all, to kill him. I wanted to punch his face so hard he would never remember who he was. I wanted to see teeth popping out of his mouth as I delivered one punch after the other.

Clothespins pinched my nipples, making me feel a constant stream of pain that emanated from there. In my mouth was a ball gag, and it had been inside of it for so long I didn't think I'd be able to close my mouth again when he next took it out.

Just thinking about that, I was wondering when he was going to do that. If I remembered correctly, he got out of his car not too long ago when he was coming back from something he had to do in the city. I didn't even know what he went to do there. All I knew was that it didn't have anything to do with me.

It happened during his session with me. He was having his fun humiliating me and pointing out again and again that I 'betrayed' him. Imagine the audacity saying something like that to my face. He was the one who betrayed me, with several whores, even.

Just thinking about that made me feel like killing myself. If only that was possible right now...

I couldn't help but think back to Elogio, who helped me so much when he could. Even when he couldn't, he was there for me. I had such an amazing night with him it was forever going to remain in my mind. He was so loving and caring, which were attributes that men like him usually didn't have. I wished I had told him that when I was still with him. It was too late for that now, though.

I had to make preparations for my next plan even though I didn't have one. All I knew was that I was getting out of here again, one way or another.

I tried to move my arms, but the chains were too sturdy. I heard them rattling, my pussy in pain. There was something stuck inside of it. I didn't know what it was, but he said that it was supposed to make it large enough for him.

He was such an idiot. We had sex before and he never needed that. That toy, which was more like a humiliation instrument, served only to make me feel more pain. It was like I had something made of needles stuck inside my vagina.

The more I moved, the more it started to prickle against the walls of my pussy, making me wince. I was having difficulty breathing, too. The room didn't have any windows, was underground, and I couldn't even see any air vents. If nobody opened the door, I was pretty sure I'd die suffocated.

I struggled against the chains as I tried to do something – anything – to get anybody's attention, but it was useless. It was likely nobody was outside of the room.

My body was also covered in bruises, cuts, and scars. Elogio enjoyed beating me like I was less than trash. I closed my eyes, took a deep breath, and tried to feel better, but it wasn't working. It wasn't like I could pretend I wasn't here. I was at the mercy of one of the most ruthless Mafia bosses in the world and everybody feared him.

Including me. I feared him and what he could do.

I was so tired. Part of the reason why I was keeping my eyes closed was that I needed to eat something – anything. Elogio hadn't given me any food for hours. It was all part of his play. He wanted to make me feel submissive. He knew that I was a good fighter and that I was brave. He wanted to break me, and it was working.

I thought I heard someone opening the door, and I started to shake my body. It was more out of fear than anything, though. My body still shaking, I was surprised when I felt a hand grabbing my chin. I opened my eyes right away as I saw the face of the man I most hated. Elogio was back and even though I wanted to kill him, I was relieved that he was back. At least I wasn't going to die suffocated.

"You waited for me."

I had no idea what he was talking about. It wasn't like I could get out of the room. He was always crazy like that sometimes. Perhaps he was thinking he was funny, but I didn't see anything funny about it.

I narrowed my eyes slightly when he took the ball gag out of my mouth. I could finally speak and yet I didn't feel like doing so.

He slapped my face suddenly. I felt the pain that it made and I welcomed it. It was better than feeling tired all the time. It made me feel alive, which was the opposite reason he expected from it.

"I didn't wait for you. You can be sure of something I'll do one day – I'll kill you."

He chuckled, slapping my cheek again. "I don't think so, darling. You have no choice anymore, and my men will be more cautious from now on. They'll think twice before accepting anything from you. Not to mention that they already know what I do to people who disappoint me."

"And why don't you just kill me already? I wish my father was dead, too."

"I'll deal with your father when the time is right. Right now, he doesn't pose any danger to me. He's nothing more than trash, just like you."

I gritted my teeth. It was difficult to find out who was the bigger asshole.

He undid his belt and then it fell to the floor. He took off his pants and then his underwear, making me feel shivers running down my spine. The last thing I wanted to see was what my eyes were seeing now.

His cock, and it was disgusting.

He wrapped his fingers around it, making it bounce up and down right in front of my face. I looked up, finding his eyes. "If you put that in my mouth, it won't come out the same."

He curled up the corner of his lips. "Oh, my darling. I'm just waiting for you to do that. I want to see how brave you really are. I want to find out how much you want to die. And believe me that I'll kill you if you do that. If you hurt me, I'll hurt everyone you know, including your little sister."

I bit my lower lip. I didn't think he was going to remember her. My little sister was everything to me and the most important person in the world. She was the only one who never wronged me. I didn't think he was going to use her against me.

"If you touch her, I'll kill you too. I'll do much more than that. I'll make your life a living hell."

He gave his cock a couple of strokes. I had no idea how he was feeling about this, what exactly was going on in his mind, but I had a hint. The smile on his face was telling me what I needed to know.

He was aroused by the fact that I was still putting up with his humiliation of me. He was enjoying it, and I needed to do something about that.

He put his hand on the back of my head as he grabbed it.

"Talking with you is fun and all, but I came here for something else." Just as he finished saying that and when I thought he was going to make me suck him off, the door opened.

The man that was behind the doorway took a couple of steps back as he noticed what he was interrupting. "Sorry, boss, but there's something you need to know about Roman. He's back in the country and wants to kill you."

Elogio groaned, putting his clothes back on. He caressed my forehead before saying, "Don't worry about me. I'll be back soon and with great news. I've been talking with your father about marrying your little sister to my brother. I'm sure he'll accept it."

It wasn't like my father could say no to that, too. My blood was boiling in my veins. I wanted to kill that asshole and turn his life into a living hell.

I was going to have to wait for my revenge.

CHAPTER 10

I found her. She was in a room underground and beaten up pretty badly. I wanted to go in there and save her, but I couldn't. Not right now. One good thing about this place was that there were so many people living and working here it was unlikely I was going to get caught.

My heart was in my throat and my blood was bubbling. I couldn't stop thinking about all the horrible things Elogio kept doing to her. Today was different, though. I didn't know anything about any Roman guy, but it appeared that Elogio had been waiting for him to come back, and now he was going to kill him.

I was slinking down one of the corridors underground when he came out of her room in a hurry. He didn't even give me a second look. He didn't even look at me, for that matter. One moment he was on the property and the next he was somewhere else. He was in his car, which he preferred driving himself, and now I knew I had some free time with Naida.

Getting into her room was going to be a little complicated, though. Elogio was in a hurry when he left, but he didn't forget one important little thing – leaving someone he trusted right outside the room, and he was seated on a wooden chair.

His hands were holding a Playboy magazine, which he was flipping the pages over and over again as he admired the girls on the pages. I couldn't help but feel disgusted at that. I never liked porn, and much less Playboy.

I padded over to him without showing him any signs of what I thought about that. My face was expressionless and professional. He looked up, closing his magazine as he stood up.

"The boss wants me to check up on her," I said, tipping up my chin. It was important to make him think that I really had been living here for some time. The men that worked for Elogio didn't leave the place often, and they all slept and ate here. This place was more than a fortress. It was a prison. A prison made just for Naida…

I couldn't tolerate someone getting tortured, and she'd been going through hell recently. I was going to do something about that, no matter what happened to me. As long as I managed to get her out of there, I'd feel at peace. I'd even die with a smile on my face.

"Sorry, but you're not allowed into the room."

"The boss specifically told me to check up on her. Do you really want to get on his bad side?"

He bit his bottom lip, eventually opening the door.

"You can go in, but only because I think the boss didn't have enough time to tell me everything. Get in there, make sure she's okay, and give her some of the food you brought with you. The boss doesn't want to see her dead."

Thinking that she was probably hungry and thirsty made me feel a huge urge to kill that asshole that did this to her. Elogio wasn't going to live the rest of his life to its fullest potential. I was promising myself that, and it was something that I was going to make happen, one way or another.

I didn't say anything else, getting into the room and closing the door. The only light bulb in the room was already turned on. The light was white and not very inviting, showing me the person I came here for. She was on the other side of the room, her head lowered. Naida was chained to one of the walls and was on her knees. I felt so sorry for her I was already planning our escape route, and it was going to work. She didn't have to worry about that.

I walked over to her, stopped in front of her, and then got on one knee. I pulled out one of the apples I brought for her and waited. I was waiting to see if she was going to lift her head and show me that she still recognized me. But her head was still lowered and she wasn't giving me any signs, other than her breathing, that she was alive.

I didn't know what I felt more strongly, if it was the urge to kill that asshole who did this to her or having her in my arms again. *Naida, I'm going to avenge you. I'm going to do everything in my power to show him that he committed one of the worst sins in the world.*

"Naida..." I said, my voice low to not draw suspicions. The walls in here weren't thick enough and the sound carried through them like they were paper sheets.

She finally lifted her head, for a moment looking like she didn't recognize me.

"Velio? Is that really you?" She eventually asked, her voice sounding so throaty and weak. I couldn't help but feel sorry for her. She shouldn't be going through something like this. A woman of her caliber should be chilling out on a beach somewhere, drinking coconut water...

"Yes, it's me. I came here to rescue you," I said, not knowing exactly how I was going to do that. The only thing I knew was that it needed to be done. "And I brought you something to eat."

"What...?" She said, looking down and spotting the apple in my hand. I took it to her mouth and she took a bite. As she chewed it, I couldn't help but wish I could get her out of here right at this moment.

Now that Elogio wasn't on the property, it was my best shot at doing that, wasn't it? I didn't know, but looking over my shoulder and already thinking of all the possibilities, I supposed it was worth a try. The only problem with that was that Naida was too weak, and there wasn't much I could do about that.

When she finished her apple and a couple of other things I gave her, I asked, "Do you think you can walk? Elogio isn't here anymore. We should leave now."

"What?" She said, looking confused. I knew why she was that

way. She was so tired she couldn't even properly process the things happening around her.

The more I thought about it, the more I hated that guy. He needed to suffer so much for the things he did.

I pulled out of my pocket a key that took me a while to find. It was the key that was going to open her chains.

When I showed her the key, she blinked twice, showing me she was even more confused.

"Is that the key to my chains?" She asked.

I nodded, opening a happy smile.

"It is. I'm going to get you out of here, one way or another. We are not going to have a better opportunity than this."

"Wait, what-" she was saying when I was already removing the chains and putting her clothes on her. She couldn't walk out of the room naked, of course.

When she was dressed and looking almost like the person I had seen in Italy, I hugged her tightly. I felt that it was something that needed to be done, that I wanted to do almost as much as I wanted to get her out of here.

She hugged me back, even though I could tell her arms were weaker. I pulled back, looked into her eyes, and then kissed her. My eyes went down as I realized that, before dressing her, I had to pull that thing out of her vagina, whatever it was called.

I looked around the room, making note of all the torture devices that Elogio used on her. He was a monster. Even for Mafia standards, he was one of the most despicable men I knew. If I ever had the chance, I'd kill him.

"I missed you so much. I know we barely know each other, but you are the only man who ever showed me kindness."

I caressed her cheek, stepping away from her as I said, "Be ready for my signal. I'm going to create a distraction and then I'll be back. When that happens, I'll put you on Elogio's motorcycle, and then we'll ride off."

And just when I was going to open the door, she grabbed my hand and said, "I'll be waiting here. I trust you."

I gave her one last kiss and then walked out of the room, more determined now than I had ever been.

CHAPTER 11

Naida

Pacing back and forth in the room, I was still waiting for the signal. How many minutes had it been since he walked out? I didn't know. One of the bigger downsides about being in this room underground was that I had no sense of the passage of time. It was like everything was frozen in time, or that everything was happening at the same time.

I was biting my nails. I was so nervous that he'd get himself killed and I wouldn't have enough time to save him. I was hugging myself as it was basically the only thing I could do right now to make myself feel better. I could almost pretend he was the one hugging me right now.

I wanted to be in his arms again. The fact that he came all the way from Italy meant that he really loved me. He was a good man with a good heart in a world that didn't deserve him.

I was so happy that I wasn't chained to the wall anymore and that I could walk around in the room. That didn't mean I didn't have to be careful anymore, though. I was pretty sure that the guard who was 'taking care of me' was still outside of the room. He could still hear almost everything going on in here.

For a moment, when I thought I heard his signal, nothing happened. Everything was calm and silent on the property. I sighed, getting more and more nervous. I kept thinking that my savior was going to die.

And then, I felt something shaking the ground. It was an explosion. I just heard it. It was like someone dropped an atomic bomb on the property. I almost lost my balance and had to reposition myself by throwing my weight against the wall.

That had to be his signal, I thought. Now I only had to wait for him to come here.

My heart was in my throat as I heard guards going everywhere on the property, saying things like how lost they were about what was happening. They had no idea. They were ready to start shooting their attackers, but they couldn't see anything.

I could hear hurried footsteps going left and right in the hallway in front of the basement. I was hoping that one of them belonged to my savior, but time was passing and none of those footsteps were stopping. They were just guys who worked for Elogio and were doing everything in their power to find out what happened.

They were still in disarray when, finally, the door opened and I took two steps backward as I realized it wasn't Velio. It was someone else and he was the guard that had been outside the room.

He rushed over to me as he tried to grab my arm.

"I don't know what the fuck's happening here, but I'm pretty sure that it's someone looking for you. I'm not about to let him get you out of here. I know how important you are to the boss."

"Stay away from me!" I shouted when a bullet exploded his head. I couldn't fight him because I was too tired – way more so than when I was in that barrel in Italy.

His body fell limp to the floor, his submachine gun stopping right in front of my feet. I picked it up as I realized someone else was coming into the room. I was shocked when I realized it was Velio, who had a serious expression on his face.

He grabbed my arm as we stormed out of the basement.

"We don't have much time! We need to get out of here right now."

And we were, although I didn't think it was going to be easy. We just reached the main hall of the property when we realized there were too many guards there for us to kill. Not to mention that they were doing a sweep of the mansion and were going to find us soon if we didn't do something about it.

I was behind Velio when he looked over his shoulder. He grabbed his grenade as he pulled the pin out.

"I was hoping I was going to have to use this later. Be prepared to run with me. I think the whole house is going to collapse."

I nodded, feeling more nervous than I had ever been in my life. The reason for that was because, this time, I only had him to help me right now, and I was tired and weak. I was much weaker than the first time I escaped this place.

He threw the grenade into the main hall and when it exploded and the pillars started to collapse, we jumped out. The whole mansion was crumbling as we realized we had a clear path toward one of the garages. The door was open. Elogio always left his garages open. He was always careless like that, which was one of the reasons why I managed to flee from this place at that time. It was also one of the reasons why Velio's crazy plan was working.

"Let's go!" He shouted and we sprinted over there, getting on the motorcycle. We put on the helmets as I hugged him from behind. I tossed the submachine gun away because I couldn't use it right now. Not to mention that, looking behind my shoulder, I could see that all the guards in the mansion were in complete disarray.

They didn't even notice that we were already leaving.

When Velio fired up the engine and we rode off, though, I heard one of them shouting, "It's them! They are leaving!"

We heard shots aimed at us. I ducked as we raced through the trees and then eventually got to one of the freeways. I peeked behind my shoulder to see if any of them managed to keep chasing us, but it appeared that we were in the clear. I couldn't see any other cars or motorcycles coming after us.

"I think we are okay."

"Not yet. There's still the part about finding a place to hole up at."

"I hope you find a good one, then."

He looked over his shoulder and I could see his smile through his helmet. "We will, don't worry."

He took us to a small village in the middle of nowhere. I said 'in the middle of nowhere' because not even I could figure out where we were. We didn't have our phones with us and the place didn't have internet. The clerk at the front desk was a grumpy old woman who handed us the keys, and soon we were opening the door of our room.

When I stepped inside it, I felt like I was on the moon. My body felt so free and light. I couldn't think of anything else that wasn't loving the man who was with me, and there was so much to get to know about him, too. I knew that it was going to take a while, but he could learn a lot about me, and I, about him.

He wrapped me in his arms, pushing me against one of the walls. His lips were right in front of my face. He cocked his head slightly as he kissed me, our kiss passionate and very slow.

I could feel the beating of his heart against my chest. After everything that happened, finally being able to relax felt like something alien to me. Now that we were here and out of reach of any mafia, I could finally relax and feel that my life wasn't in danger all the time, even though that couldn't be true.

He pulled back, his eyes looking into mine and telling me a million things through them.

"I'm so happy we're together again."

"I'm happy, too," I breathed, taking off his shirt and feeling his bare chest with my hands. Again, I couldn't help but wonder about the stories behind his scars and tattoos. I was hoping he would tell me them one day, but that was a moment for another time.

Right now, I just wanted to love him.

I pushed him down against the bed. Climbing up on top of him, I started to kiss and love his lips again. I groaned as he snuck one of his fingers under my pants, finding the crack of my ass. He played with it for a little while and then pulled down my pants.

Making love with Velio again? I didn't think it was going to happen while we were still on the run, but I was happy that it was. I kneaded his skin, pinched his nipples, and groaned when he started to fumble my asscheeks.

He was so hungry to be inside of me again.

CHAPTER 12

Velio

Gosh, my blood was pumping in my veins. I ripped the shirt off of her body, turning ourselves around so that I was on top of her. Her bra was the next thing to go, and then I was mauling on her boobs like this was the end of the world.

She moaned so loudly when I pinched one of her nipples and then nibbled on it, drawing this out until she was already orgasming. It happened so fast that it could only be so because of this one reason – she was too stressed and needed this moment to release her stress.

I licked her right boob and then moved down, finding her panties. I took them off and she wrapped her legs around me. I still had my pants on, but I was pretty sure they weren't going to remain there for much longer. Her hands were, after all, already looking for ways to take it off me as soon as possible.

I moved down again, licking her little rosebud. She tightened the hug of her legs on me, bringing me further down. I could feel the smell of her snatch, and it was delicious. It contrasted nicely with the darker tone of her skin.

I groped her body, finding all the curves. She was perfect. Her skin was so smooth and soft. I'd be kissing it and feeling it like this for all of eternity, if it was possible. I was pretty sure she was thinking the same way about it, too.

I put one of her legs over my shoulders, my hand under her

thigh as I started playing with her pussy lips. She was so ready. I could see her wetness glinting against the soft lighting in the room. Her breathing was slow and heavy, and I could tell that this moment was quite taxing on her.

"I love you so much," I said, feeling as if we were made for one another. I didn't know where that was even coming from, just that it felt right. It felt right to be saying that I was in love with Naida even though we didn't know each other well.

Was someone going to say that there was something wrong with that? I didn't think so. I focused on loving her clit, playing with her folds as she orgasmed a second time. And when her orgasm was all over the bedsheets and on her lips, I licked it off with a dirty smile on my face.

Then, I kissed her again and she didn't mind that she was tasting her own orgasm. She actually smiled as if to tell me she liked it. Moments later, I turned her around and I positioned myself so that my dick was going into her mouth.

She opened it wide, welcoming it. I started to thrust my hips as I continued to lick her little rosebud. Gosh, giving it long licks and then short, quick ones was the way to go. She was moaning so loudly she was making me wonder how she hadn't come a third time yet.

I was almost there, too. My body and especially my balls were so hot I felt like I was in a sauna. Her orgasm was delicious and I couldn't stop licking it up.

Her whole body was trembling in pleasure. When our pace started to slow down, I decided to do something different. I pulled her to me after flipping her around on the bed. I noticed that the bedsheets were soaked in our sweat, and knowing that was good.

I made her stay on all fours on the bed. I lowered my body as I started to lick her asshole. One lick after the other, I softened it up. It was still a little tight, but I was pretty sure I could get inside of it. When I was pounding in and out of her, I knew it was going to feel like I was in heaven.

"Oh, gosh. This is so good," she groaned as I lined up my cock to her asshole. It was open and tight for me, I noticed as I started to nudge it. I grabbed her waist more tightly as I thrust in with more force. Moments later, I was inside of her and it was the best thing in the world. She was so tight and hot I couldn't imagine myself pulling out until I was ready.

I started to thrust in and out of her, doing so slowly. I was savoring this moment for everything it was and for everything it meant. Naida was groaning and moaning as she matched my pace. There was nothing better than doing this with someone that was already used to how I liked to do things.

"How are you feeling? Better already?" I asked, my lips so near her ear I wanted to nibble on her earlobe, but I didn't do it. I was waiting for her answer and I didn't want to distract her.

"Better than ever before," she responded before I increased my pace and she started to match it again. The most striking thing was that I was going to come inside of her rectum and it was even better than doing it in her pussy.

Moments later, my dick erupted and I started to shoot out rope after rope of my sperm. She arched her back and groaned louder than before as she came with me. There was nothing better than climaxing at the same time with the first person I truly loved.

I stayed inside of her moments after my cock was flaccid again.

I kissed the nape of her neck before finally pulling out and falling on the bed. She lied down on it, hugging me. Our eyes met again and I could tell she was only thinking positive things about me.

"That was amazing," she said, her hand running over the side of my body. She wanted to feel as much of me as she could.

"You were amazing. I knew it was going to be incredible, but I didn't think it was going to be like that. I'm still trying to catch my breath."

A second later, she asked, "How are we going to flee from the country?"

"Flee from the country? What do you mean?"

"We can't stay here. After what we did, Elogio will be hunting us down until he kills us."

"Don't worry about it. I'll figure something out."

She bit her lower lip before she said, "I have a little sister who's still living with my father. I think Elogio will come for her to hurt me."

I cupped her face with my hand. "Don't worry about that. We still have time. Tell me where she lives with your father and I'll rescue her."

"It won't be so easy. Elogio and my father have several men willing to die for them. You'll have to fight against an army."

"I'm willing to do that. If it means keeping you safe and happy, then it's worth it. It's worth everything."

She smiled softly again, allowing me to feel the smell of her mouth. It was everything I thought it still was. The more I thought about it, the more I realized she was still the same woman I knew. Being in Elogio's grasp this whole time didn't change her at all. She was still as strong as she had always been.

"Thanks. I suppose there's no time to waste, then."

I looked up at the ceiling, thinking about it. Naida was right. Elogio probably already knew about what happened and was already coming for us. I imagined that her sister lived somewhere nearby, which meant we should have enough time to rescue her.

I kissed her again before saying, "You're right. There's no time to waste. We need to go there."

She groaned, jumping off the bed. We put our clothes on, got back on the motorcycle, and then when I thought I was going to fire up the engine, I noticed that one of Elogio's guards was already patrolling the area. He was looking for us and even though I doubted he knew my face, I was pretty sure he knew hers.

I gritted my teeth. This was going to be harder than I thought, but looking behind my shoulder and remembering how well I was bonding with her, I knew there was nothing else I would rather do right now. Even though that meant risking my life more than it was already in danger, it was better than not doing anything.

Not to mention that Naida would never forgive me if I didn't do the right thing. I twisted the handlebars of the motorcycle as we rode out of there. Blowing smoke up behind me, I was thinking about just one thing – making sure that Naida and her sister were going to be okay.

NAIDA'S EPILOGUE

I couldn't be any happier that Velio did so much for me. I was with my sister, on a hill overlooking Chicago. From up here, we could see pretty much everything. We had to keep being on the run, for now, but that was okay. We'd been in worse situations before, and I was pretty sure that we were going to make it out, no matter what happened.

I was holding her hand. She was my little sister, but a little grown up now. She was looking up at the sky, her eyes closed as she took in the fresh smell of the alpine trees.

Her hand was soft and comforting. I loved her as my sister, and I'd do anything for her.

"I don't know how you managed to get me out of there without getting yourselves killed, but you still did. I'm so happy for us."

She turned, looking at me.

"I'd do anything for you, and you know that. It's no surprise that I did what I did."

I glanced to the side, finding Velio seated on his car's roof and cleaning up his pistol. He was still making plans to kill Elogio and I was trying to convince him that he didn't need to do it. After all, as long as we managed to flee far enough from Elogio, he wouldn't be able to find us. We'd be far away from everything, where no one could ever find us.

That was a promise I was making to myself anyway.

She let go of her hand, narrowing her eyes. "You need to teach me how to fight. I want to be able to protect myself."

I widened my eyes, finding it surprising she said that. She

wanted to lose her innocence and learn how to fight like I did? I wasn't going to do that. No way. I wasn't going to ruin the sweet person she was.

"No, I'm not going to do that."

"Why not? Do you think I can defend myself the way I am? I need to be stronger, or else someone will hurt me."

I grabbed her shoulders. "I'll be there to protect you every day. Don't worry about that. I'll always be by your side."

She took my hands off of her shoulders. As she turned around, she said, "I know you want only what's best for me, but things don't work that way. It's not that simple. If my father or Elogio come for us and you aren't there, there'll be nothing I can do."

She was right, but still, I wasn't used to the idea of training her. I still thought of her as my little sister, and she pretty much was. She was growing, but that still didn't mean I had to start looking at her differently.

Destini grabbed my hand as she said, "I'm going to be fine, really. It's just a precaution. I won't harm anyone with what you teach me unless it's necessary."

"I know, but it's still difficult. I'll think about it, okay?"

She let go of my hand and opened a smile. "Thanks, big sis. I knew I could count on you."

"Something the matter?" A booming voice asked from my side, making me snap my head where it came from. It was Velio, who had finished cleaning his gun. He was looking at us with worried eyes.

"It's just that Destini wants me to train her."

"Sounds like a great idea. Maybe I could help, too," he said, opening a soft smile.

"No, you won't."

"Why not?" Destini asked, putting herself between me and the person I wanted to marry. I never considered myself Elogio's wife, so it felt right to be thinking that way about Velio.

"Because it would be dangerous."

"Urgh, you're so frustrating sometimes, sis," Destini walked away from us, crossing her arms.

I was going to her when Velio put his hand on my waist, pulling me to him. He locked his lips with mine. His lips were really sweet and I couldn't imagine myself without him. We were still getting to know each other, but there was no denying that we were made for one another.

He pulled his head back as he caressed the side of my face.

"I'm going to be there all the way with her. She's a little pissed right now, but she'll feel a lot better when she can better protect herself. Do it for her and I'm sure you'll feel a lot better, too."

I sighed, kissing him again. I was still conflicted about it, but there was no denying he was right about something – I should do it for Destiny. If something happened and I couldn't be there to protect her, then she would.

"I love you so much. You already make me feel so much better about it."

He gave me a gentle smile. "I knew you were going to see reason. We'll start slow. I'll show her how to fight hand-to-hand properly and then we'll teach her how to shoot a gun."

"What about Elogio? Are you still going to try killing him?"

He narrowed his eyes slightly. "Yes, that's out of the question. He needs to be killed. His whole family needs to be. Otherwise, we won't live happily and we'll be on the run all the time. I don't think that you want that for us and the baby, right?"

I looked down, my hand roaming over my big belly. He got me pregnant while I was still in Italy. A couple of months into the pregnancy and I was already feeling some of the effects of it. Nausea, weird urges to eat certain foods, and that sort of thing. Being pregnant was awesome and tiresome at the same time. I couldn't wait until I was holding the baby in my arms, though.

I pecked his lips again and then we headed over to Destini to tell her the 'good' news. It was time to move as far away from America as we could.

VELIO'S EPILOGUE

"**I** told you it was going to happen and, frankly, I'm happy that it did."

"You're happy that your brother is behind bars? You're a sick idiot. That's what you are. Can't believe you ended up marrying a nigger."

I felt my blood boiling in my veins. I didn't know why he called me and why he was even still talking to me. I ceased all contact with him after escaping Elogio. My focus was on him right now. I was going to get my revenge, no matter the cost.

"Say that again and I'll go there and kill you myself, Carlo."

"You didn't do anything when they came to lock me up. I thought you had my back, but I misjudged you. When it comes down to it, you only care about yourself and not the family."

"The family didn't give me anything. I had to fight for all of it myself, and you were one of the few who showed me that I was wrong about them from the beginning. It wasn't worth it. It never was."

"You're such a piece of shit you make me feel like busting out of this prison just to kill you."

And after he said that, I realized there was no more point in talking to him. I ended the call and shoved the phone back into the cradle. I turned around, my blood boiling, and noticed that the most beautiful woman in the world was right behind me. We were in our house, and it was perfect and beautiful. We finally had enough support to live a normal life without having to worry about Elogio all the time. I was trying to go straight now, just like she made me promise.

"I told you that picking up the call was a waste of time."

"I thought he could change or had changed, even if only a little. I'm not disappointed, but it still hurts. When we were little, we used to play together so much, and he really was someone I looked up to. Not anymore, I guess. Now he'll have to live knowing that his brother is leading a much happier life. I'm not going to be locked up. I never will."

"I know, love," she said, wrapping her arms around me and pulling me down for a hot, wet kiss. Her belly was even bigger now and her cravings were growing more intense. One of the other things I was happy about was that we had enough for all of that and a lot more. Money wasn't an issue for us anymore.

"I hope he never walks out of prison. I don't like to think what he'd do."

"Let's not worry about him. I think there's something you're going to like and that's going to make you forget everything about him."

I purred against her. "Hmm, I like the sound of that. Show me what that is."

Naida grabbed my hand and took me to the second floor of our house. I scanned the environment outside for anything suspicious, but there wasn't anything. Just trees, more trees, a river snaking through them, my guards patrolling the perimeter, and that sort of thing. Overall, I couldn't be happier that we were living in such a peaceful place. We could even hear our footsteps.

When Naida stopped in front of a room with a different, special kind of door, I knew what she was talking about. I wasn't home as often as I'd like, so I wasn't in the loop regarding the reformation of this room. It was supposed to be the baby's room and it was connected to ours.

In case anything happened to our little one, we'd be able to get there in no time and help him.

And yes, it was going to be a boy. The door was adorned and painted to help make everything look more inviting for our little one. I was pretty sure that, the first time he looked at it, he'd open a huge smile on his face.

Naida looked at me and said, "It's finally ready. You're going to love the final result."

She opened the door and stepped into the room. There was a crib, toys, ornaments hanging from the ceiling and the walls, the walls themselves were painted with scenes from cartoons, and the whole place had such a sweet smell. The baby was still a few weeks from being born, but there was no denying that Naida liked thinking about everything. It was one of the reasons why she was preparing everything for when our family was bigger.

I turned around and said, "It's beautiful. I knew you were going to make it look perfect." I said that because Naida was the one who chose everything from the beginning. She chose the color for the walls, the design of the paintings, how big the crib was going to be, and, well, who could have guessed that someone as tough as her knew how to decorate rooms?

I kissed her again and said, "It's amazing. It's so pretty I'm already thinking we should reformulate our room, too. I never thought that our room looked bland, but now that I see how good you are at doing this…"

We kissed one more time, our bodies pressing against each other.

"I know and I'd be more than happy to do that for us, especially after seeing how this room turned out. I hope we can get rid of Elogio as soon as possible so that we don't have to worry about anything."

"We will. Don't worry. He's tough, but I'm joining up with Roman and we should be able to sniff him out before it's too late. We're not letting him escape the country."

She looked into my eyes and murmured something that was forever going to be ingrained in it.

"Thank you."

The End

Dive into the rest of the series by reading these books:

1. His Accidental Triplets
2. His Sweet Captive
3. His Stolen Bride
4. His Accidental Baby
5. His Secret Triplets
6. His Fleeing Single Mom
7. His Fake Marriage

Lastly, leave a review if you liked this story. Thank you!

LOOKING FOR ACCIDENTAL TRIPLETS?

His Accidental Triplets: BWWM Dark Mafia Romance

Ida

I could already feel the ogling of the customers, stepping into the main room of The Houz and hoping that I could get through the crowd as quickly as possible. But, looking at all these people standing in front of me, I could tell that doing that wasn't going to be simple.

I felt some tightness in my chest. It wasn't that I didn't like big crowds, but that this strip club, in particular, made me feel like ripping the flesh off my body.

I turned my head slightly to the right, finding a woman sashaying down the stage like she owned it. I couldn't help but feel a huge wave of repulsion, asking myself what she thought she was doing with her life.

I'd seen so many times what she did after The Houz closed. She went out to the alley in the back and allowed men to abuse her for some cash. I'd never say that I felt proud of my job, but at least I didn't have to do… the things she did for money.

My salary was just enough to survive, and I wouldn't say she was doing much better than I was. Quite the contrary, I was assuming. She probably made as much as I did, without the benefit of not having to sell out for some dollars.

If I could, I wouldn't be working here. I would be kicking back on the beach, sipping some coconut water, and making plans for the next luxury car I would buy.

I sighed, pushing through the crowd while holding a heavy bucket of water and a mop. I needed to reach the makeup room, or dressing room, or whatever it was called. In essence, it was where the 'performers' went to retouch their makeup and fix their hair.

Try as they might to look pretty, they couldn't change their souls. They sold them to the devil a long time ago. And while part of me blamed them for that, I knew that it wasn't that simple. Our failing economy and inflation were driving people to do the stupidest of things.

But that was enough rambling. I needed to keep pushing through this dancing, drinking crowd and reach that room. Upon getting there, I needed to make it look squeaky clean.

It wasn't that I thought I could really make that happen, though. The makeup room was usually dirty, and more often than not the girls that worked here took their clients there when they couldn't wait until they could find a more appropriate place.

Chicago had so many motels and yet people still had sex there. I didn't know what was usually going on in their minds, but it surely wasn't anything pretty.

Again, I pushed the rambling away and thought how ironic it was that a virgin woman like myself was working in a place like this. And being 21 now, with my parents having died a long time ago, I had to remember I wasn't in this situation because of my fault.

Or, maybe it kind of was. I was saving myself for the right man. So many of my friends – not the ones from church – kept insisting that I was making the wrong decision, that I was missing out, but they couldn't understand my motivations.

I grew up watching my mom and father being the happiest couple ever before they were killed, and they followed the same path I was.

A tear rolled down my cheek, remembering the day they died. My sister wasn't with me then, and I had to run back home to comfort her. Her crying made me break down too, and at that moment, I cried like a dam had burst.

Ever since then, I promised to keep Dalanie safe, and that's what I was doing. Even now, when she kept making it pretty clear she didn't like me one bit.

But she was only 17. I was pretty sure that, with time, she was going to realize I was the only thing standing between her and a life of complete misery, living in the streets and having to depend on other people to make ends meet.

Nevertheless, it wasn't like that was much different than what I was doing now, I thought with a frown.

I exhaled in pure relief when I finished pushing through the crowds and just when I thought I was safe, I felt something liquid and wet splashing on my shirt.

I snapped in the direction it came from, finding a white man in his early twenties with a grin on his face, holding a slightly-turned glass in his hand.

"You should be watching where you're going, ni-" he was saying before someone bumped into him, making his hand finish turning the glass until all of the beer in it splashed on my shirt.

On other occasions, when I was still starting out here, I would be fuming at what he did. But I'd be lying if I said this was the first time this was happening.

I shook my head, still holding the bucket with water in one hand and the mop in the other. I put the water bucket on the floor, rubbed my hand over my shirt in a futile attempt to dry the beer, and then turned and tuned that man out of my mind.

He was a racist jerk and, in this establishment, there were plenty of people like him. I needed their money to keep surviving in here, though, and it wouldn't be good for my boss if I insulted him, even though that idiot had almost called me the n-word.

I wasn't going to pretend it didn't bother me. It did – a lot, and I was already feeling my blood boiling. If I didn't need this job at all,

I'd already be slapping the shit out of him and kicking him-

Oh God, what the hell was that thought that was crossing my mind now? I thought before opening the door of the dressing room and stepping into it.

Just not having to listen to the full volume of the music they played in the main room was very relieving. They played those kinds of shitty songs to keep their clients in some kind of haze in their minds, thinking about nothing but sex.

Alcohol and sex. What could really go wrong in a place like this?

As soon as my eyes scanned the room, I found what I was looking for. Some kind of weird goo on the floor, and it was probably the sperm of a man with a woman's bodily fluids mixed in it.

The thing itself made me feel a lot of repulsion, urging me to step out of this room right away. And it wasn't even empty either, I noticed, finding some girls standing not too far from me, talking among themselves.

In here, in The Houz, I was a nobody, and it wasn't like that would ever change. If anything, the women that worked here were going to keep thinking that way about me, looking down on me all the time...

Roman

My brother was standing on the other side of the desk, leaning against the wall and putting his head on his forearm. He was still chuckling and laughing, like he thought that what was happening here was some kind of joke.

"Oh, man. You really should have seen the look on your face when she told you how old she was."

"I really thought that she was in her early twenties, and then she showed me her ID, and it turned out she was almost forty."

"Yup, that kind of thing happens."

"Not in my world, though. I like knowing the age of the women I meet."

"Some of them fake it pretty damn well," he said, straightening his neck and walking until he put his hands on my desk. "You're really hellbent on finding the right woman for this job, aren't you? Even though that doesn't really matter."

"To make this business really work, I need only the best of the best," I stated. And lowering my voice, I added, "It's the only way to be successful. Without that, we would only be wasting our time."

"I know, I know," he said, pushing himself off the desk and then stepping to the door. He was the one sorting the right candidates that managed to get here, after going through a selection filter I designed for this purpose.

Looking at my brother was like looking at my reflection in a mirror that changed my clothes. He looked just like me. He even tried to maintain the same body shape, going with me to the gym so that we could work out together.

He was my twin, having been born at about the same time as me. Well, to be honest, I was a little older than he was, but a difference of a couple of minutes never really meant much when we were growing up.

And through the door stepped someone that I knew, right away, couldn't even be 18 yet. What she was doing here at the Soul Groove, I didn't know and I didn't want to know.

I was going to have to have a long talk with the men that were supposed to be selecting these girls for the position I was looking to fill. I stressed out often enough that we weren't taking underage girls – at all.

I'd already had problems of a similar nature before, and right now I wanted to keep our operations obfuscated to the authorities. It was the only way to finish laundering the money we got from that bank heist.

The news channels were still talking about it, months later. And the feds managed to jail only a few of us, who were our scapegoats.

"Sergei, get her out of here right away. I'm going to have a long talk with Gleb about how serious he's taking his job."

But Sergei wasn't a man that usually took orders from me without spinning them to his own benefit, already opening a wide smile and annoying me.

"Why don't you hear her out first?"

I didn't give him the satisfaction of answering that, already standing up quickly and striding to that young African-American while trying not to look too angry.

I could see that she was only a desperate teen trying to make some money. She was just not going to get any of it here, I re-affirmed to myself.

"You're not allowed in this establishment, whoever you are," I growled, grabbing her arm with enough confidence to make her shoot her eyes wide, but without hurting her.

"Hey, let go of me," she whined, trying to shake her arm off, but I was hellbent on getting her out of the Soul Groove before someone had the chance to record this.

One video and it would be enough to make the police come down here. I doubted they would be able to hurt my strip club without more evidence, and they wouldn't look too hard into this matter, but the less attention I had on this place, the better.

It was already located underground, without even a sign outside showing what it was that we did here. We relied on sending the right information about this place to the right people, by carefully hand picking them.

Not really the most effective and quick method of finding new customers, but we managed to find the right ones – the sharks that were willing to overspend to have a good time.

The fact that she managed to find this place was a little curious. I was already thinking about cornering her and asking her some questions later. If there was some kind of leak in how we were marketing our business, then I needed to know about it and fix it right away.

I was just storming past Sergei as I leaned to him quickly, whispering into his ear, "Find out where she leaves."

His face quickly assumed a more concerned tone, realizing that I wasn't kidding about that at all. The fact that he was my second-in-command for this operation was pretty telling.

Despite his more playful attitude and thinking that he could be better than me at something, he was a man I could trust. He was going to find out where she lived, though I didn't think that was a difficult thing to do at all. A girl like her probably took the bus or a taxi to get around. More likely the first thing than the latter, I imagined.

"You are leaving the Soul Groove right now, and not one more peep," I said through gritted teeth and was just about to turn left in the hallway when a woman, a couple of years older than her, stormed in my direction.

"Get your filthy hands off my sister right at this moment," she ordered, putting both of her hands on her waist, narrowing her eyes like she was thinking about killing me.

"Who are you?" I asked, easing my grip on her forearm, though without letting her go. I couldn't do that - not until I felt a little calmer and safer about this.

"Her sister, and more like a mother now too," she replied, striding forward and planting her hand on mine. Her grip was tight and certain, as if she was telling me that it didn't matter who I was, she was willing to put herself at risk if it meant keeping her little sister safe…

MORE BWWM DARK MAFIA AND OTHERS

SERIES ALPHA PREDATORS

1. Not my Wedding: A BWWM Dark Mafia Romance
2. Not my Vows: A BWWM Dark Mafia Romance
3. Not his Baby: A BWWM Dark Mafia Romance
4. Not my Fiancé: A BWWM Dark Mafia Romance
5. Not my Daughter: A BWWM Dark Mafia Romance

SERIES - PRETTY LIARS

1. Impossible to Choose: A BWWM Mafia Reverse Harem Romance

2. Kiss of Amnesia: Secret Baby BWWM Mafia Romance

3. Fake Boyfriend: Secret Baby BWWM Mafia Romance

4. A Baby for the Hitman: Secret Baby BWWM Mafia Romance

5. Mafia Boss's Surrogate: Amnesia BWWM Dark Mafia Romance

Other dark mafia romances:

Beg Me: An Arranged Marriage Dark Mafia Romance

Used by the Mafia Boss: A Dark Mafia Romance

Bait Me: A Dark Mafia Romance Bundle

Mafia Vassal: A Dark Italian Mafia Romance Bundle

Don't Cry: A Secret Baby Dark Mafia Romance
Seizing her Heart: A Bratva Mafia Romance Collection
Conquering my Queen: A Dark Mafia Romance Bundle

Dark Highschool Romances:

On his Knees: A Dark High School Bully Bundle
Cruel Words: A Dark High School Romance Bundle
Have no Fear: An Enemies to Lovers Academy Romance
Under his Mercy: A Dark High School Bully Romance
Lure Me: A Dark High School Bully Romance
Fallen Angel: A Dark High School Bully Romance
Stop Lying: A Dark High School and College Bundle

ABOUT THE AUTHOR

Ruthless mafiosos, gorgeous billionaires, and feisty heroines are just tiny fractions of Jolie Damman's stories. She breathes and lives dark romance, peppering each scene with intrigue and tension that sweep readers away.

A kiss isn't just that. When a characters' eyes meet another's, they speak of memories even they can't understand. It might hurt. There might be triggers, but it's all worth it in the end, and that's what Jolie Damman always believes.